Chapter 1
The Boy

— hello

Once upon a time there lived a boy called Henry.

What Henry wanted more than
anything else in the whole wide world,

more than chips,

more than a cowboy costume,

Fiona Roberton

WANTED:
The Perfect Pet

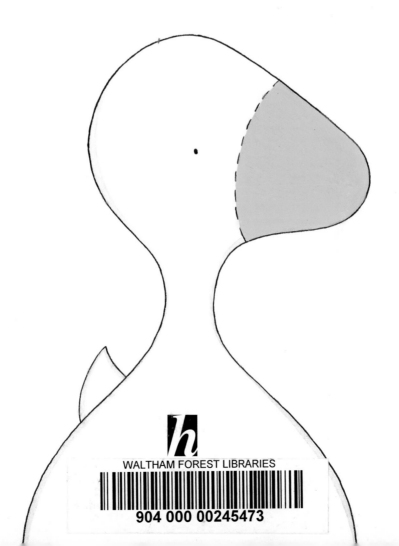

No ducks were harmed in the making of this book.

For Henry, Olivia and Anna.

First published in 2009 by Penguin Group Australia,
250 Camberwell Road, Camberwell, Vic 3124 Australia

This edition first published in 2012 by Hodder Children's Books,
a division of Hachette Children's Books, 338 Euston Road, London, NW1 3BH
An Hachette UK Company

Text and illustrations © Fiona Roberton 2009

A catalogue record of this book is available from the British Library.

ISBN: 978 1 444 90263 1

Printed in China.

www.hachette.co.uk

more than an all-expenses-paid
trip to the moon,

more, even, than
world peace itself,

was a dog.

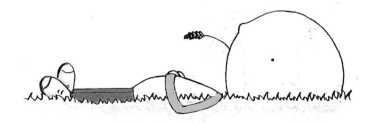

'But Henry,' said his mother, 'you already have 27 different varieties of frog, surely they are enough?'

'No,' said Henry sternly, 'they are boring.

All they do is hop and grrrribit.

I want a pet with **PERSONALITY.** I want a dog.

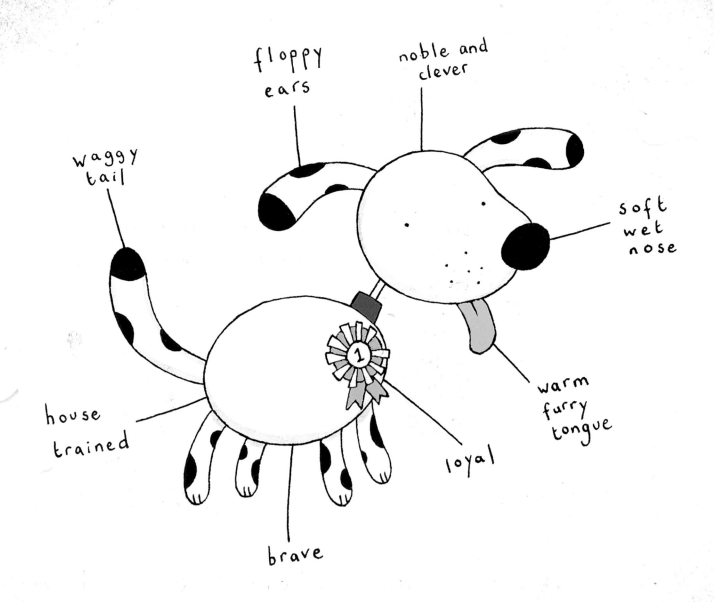

floppy ears

noble and clever

waggy tail

soft wet nose

house trained

loyal

warm furry tongue

brave

With floppy ears and a waggy tail,
and a soft wet nose, and a warm furry tongue.

A dog that can catch
balls that I throw,

that can learn
fantastic new tricks,

— SHAUSHIDGES

and that I can chase around trees.

Because it is common knowledge,' said Henry,
'that a dog is The Perfect Pet for a boy.'

So he decided to advertise.

FOR SALE:

TIME MACHINE
Settings include 'Iron Age',
'Medieval Times' and 'The
Renaissance'. Requires 4 x AA
Batteries. Hours of fun for all
the family. Parental supervision
recommended. Ages 4+.
Call: 02 - 362 4716

FOR RENT:

CASTLE, TRANSYLVANIA
3284 bedrooms, 2 bathrooms,
comfortable dungeons,
roof terrace, atmosphere of
impending doom, pit of evil,
stunning views. Booby-trapped.
Call: 02 - 376 4716

FOR HIRE:

ANGRY MOB
Available for all occasions
including weddings, political
rallies and monster lynchings.
Call: 02 - 272 3345

WOODCUTTER
Own axe, willing to travel.
Call: 07 - 786 5491

X-RAY GOGGLES
Can see through walls,
clothing, lies, space and time.
Call: 06 - 903 2672

WANTED:
THE PERFECT PET

ALSO KNOWN AS A DOG
Must have waggy tail, floppy
ears, soft wet nose and warm
furry tongue. Should be able
to learn fantastic new tricks.
Preferably house trained.
Apply in person to: Mr Henry,
The Pond House, 24 Tadpole
Lane, Little Gribblington.
Or call: 01 - 362 2341
(Evenings and weekends only).

FOR FREE:

ENCHANTED MIRROR
Always speaks the truth.
Free to good home.
Call: 09 - 782 9101

FOR SALE:

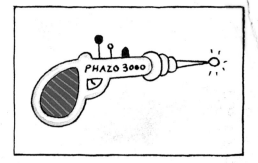

PHAZER GUN
Settings include 'Repel' and
'Stun'. Comfortable rubber
grip, hair trigger, 12 metre
range, anti-backfire mechanism.
Package includes carry case,
holster, targets and battery
recharger. Ages 8+.
Call: 01 - 482 3761

And then he waited.

Chapter 2
The Duck

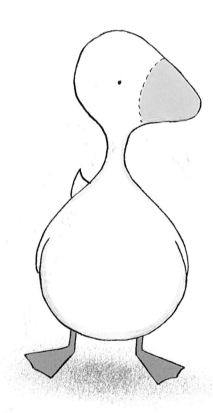

Once upon a time there lived a duck.
He didn't have a name.

He lived all alone, far, far away
at the top of a cold and windy hill.

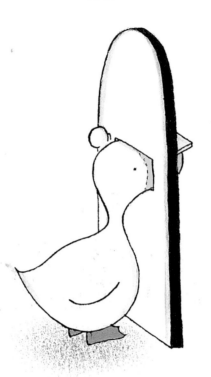

Nobody ever wrote.

Nobody ever called.

Nobody ever emailed.

He went to the movies,

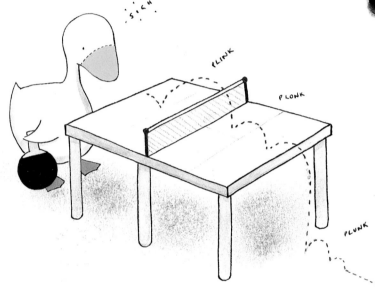

and played ping-pong,

and watched the sun rise, the sun float
about somewhere in the middle, and the
sun set, all by himself, every single day.

It wasn't much fun.

But then one day, he opened up his paper, and he saw:

'I am not a dog,' he thought, 'but if I was a dog,
I could have a friend at last.

A friend to have tea with, go to the movies with,
and play ping-pong with. A friend to watch the sun rise,
the sun float about somewhere in the middle,
and the sun set with.'

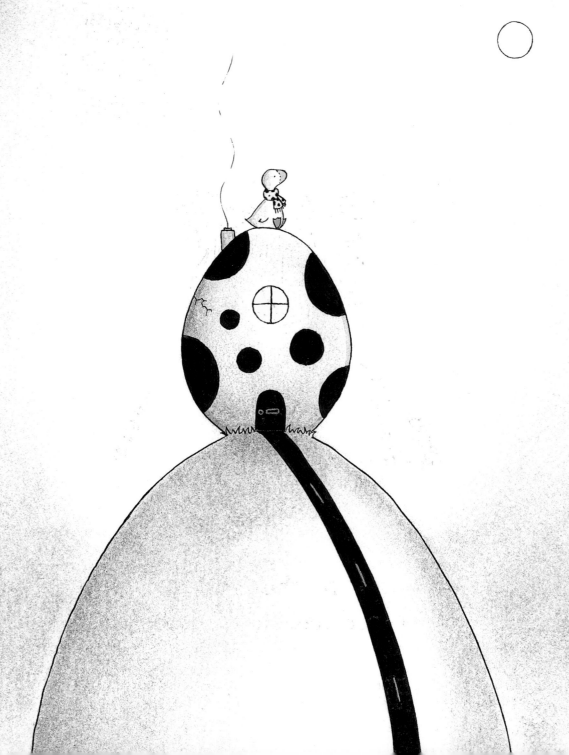

So with a pair of old socks, an egg box and some string,

perfect.

he created The Perfect Disguise.

Then he packed his things and set off on
the long journey to meet the boy.

Chapter 3
The Discovery

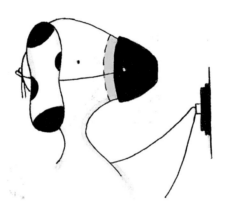

Ding Dong!

'A **dog!**'
yelled Henry.

'**Woof!**'
said the duck.

Henry had never been so excited.
The duck had never been happier. However…

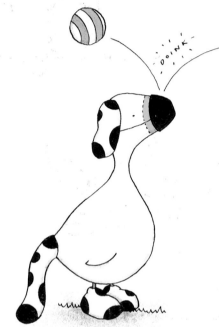

Henry's dog wasn't very
good at catching balls,

he wasn't very good at
learning new tricks,

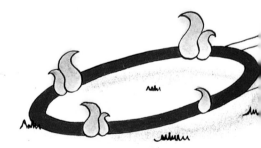

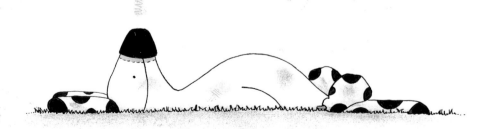

and when he chased Henry
around the trees,

he waddled…

and he slipped…

and he tripped…

and his soft wet nose and his
floppy ears and tail fell off.

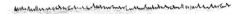

Henry was stunned. The duck slowly stood up.
A single, fat tear rolled down his beak and plopped
on the ground in front of him.

'I am sorry. I am not a dog,'
admitted the duck. 'I am just a duck.

I do not have floppy ears, or a waggy tail, or a soft wet nose, or even a warm furry tongue,' he said sadly.

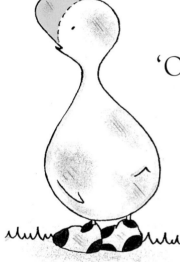

'Oh,' said Henry disappointedly. 'No, you don't.'

Henry thought for a moment. Then he picked up the duck and carried him home.

He gave the duck a nice hot bath and a cup of tea.

He took down his
Enormous Book of Incredibly
Interesting Things,

he looked under 'D',

and he made a list…

DUCK SKILLS

1. Can dive under water, can hold breath, swim and float on water. Fun in bath, at beach and useful for hunting for sunken treasure, fishing and fetching things I dropped in swimming pool.

2. Can 'FLY'. Could put on ~~aira~~ aeronautical show to earn extra pocket money. Also good skill for getting kites and frisbees and other items out of trees and next door's garden. And for drawing maps and spying on people.

3. This particular duck v.good at disguises = <u>VERY CLEVER</u>.

4. Nest building skills excellent for building forts and camps and tree houses and so on.

5. Spare feathers can be used to build indian headdresses and to tickle little sister with.

6. This duck can talk. Is rare, but not unheard of.

ALSO: Won't shed fur, get dog breath, need walking or house training. Won't eat homework, chew shoes or furniture, <u>and</u> won't pee on carpet.

↑ me   ↑ duck

...which he showed to the duck.

'So you might not be a dog,' said Henry happily, 'but you are certainly not JUST a duck. In fact, you might just be The Perfect Pet for me.

I think I'll call you Spot,' smiled Henry.

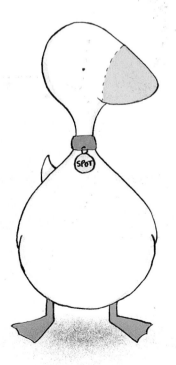

'Quack,' said Spot.

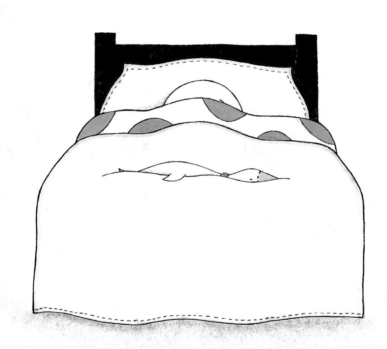